For my beloved Christian & Fernando, from Amy

Title: Aqua Dragons Sea Friends

This book is based on a series of characters "Aqua Dragons" a registered trade mark of Amy Holden and World Alive S.L.

Concept: Amy Holden

Author: Anita Loughrey

Editor: Corrinne Carter

Illustrator: Raül Arrué

Design: Shaun Grant

ISBN 978-84-617-3649-2

Legal Deposit Number DL B 1886 - 2015

1st edition Jan 2015

Printed and bound in Barcelona, Spain

Published by World Alive S.L. of Calle Navarro i Reverter 29A, 08017 Barcelona
www.aquadragons.net

Bubbles, Leela and Fin were playing near the mangrove trees.

"Look at me," Bubbles yelled, as he flipped his fins and swam backwards as fast as he could.

"Stop!" Fin yelled.

But it was too late. Bubbles swam straight into the riptide. He was swept away by the force of the water.

"We've got to save him," Leela said.

Fin tried to grab Bubbles out of the riptide.

"I can't reach," Fin said. He leant further into the current with Leela holding on to him. Swwwishhh. They too were both dragged into the riptide.

"Help!" Leela cried, as she clung to her brother's back.

The three Aqua Dragons were swept out to sea, far away from home. Bubbles scrambled against the torrent of water and clutched at some seaweed. He held on tightly. "Grab hold of my arm," Bubbles yelled at his brother and sister who were swirling towards him. Fin reached out and grasped hold of Bubble's arm. With all his strength, Bubbles flung them out of the riptide and over some rocks.

Bump! Bump! They landed on a hard shell, half hidden in the sand.
Bubbles dragged himself out of the riptide using the seaweed, then stopped in his tracks. Fin and Leela were huddled together, shaking with fear.
"Watch what you're doing!" The grouchy crab waved his claws at them.
"Don't eat us!" Leela said.

A starfish laughed at them from the rocks. "Crabby is harmless. He's so old! Eating Aqua Dragons would give him tummy ache," she said. "Go and find somewhere else to sleep Crabby."

Crabby snapped his claws and scurried sideways into a gap in the rocks.

"Hi! I'm Stella. Where are you from?" Stella the Starfish said. "I've not seen you around here before!"

The Aqua Dragons looked around them.

"I think we came from that direction." Fin pointed beyond the rocks.

"No! It was that way!" Bubbles pointed in the opposite direction.

The three Aqua Dragons glanced at each other.

"We're lost!" said Leela.

"We'll never find our way home," Leela said.
"The riptide dragged us here," Bubbles said.
Stella put an arm on Leela's shoulder. "Follow me.
I know how to get you home." She led them over
the rocks. "You have to follow the riptide." She
pointed at the fast moving current.
Stella led the way. Suddenly, Leela came to an
abrupt halt. Her brothers bumped into her.

"Oh no! Our path is blocked by a herd of
seahorses," Bubbles said.
"Seahorses eat Aqua Dragons," Fin said.
"This is the only route I know," Stella said.
"We're stranded here forever," Leela wailed.

"I know! We should go to see wise Madame Octopus," Stella said. "She will get you home."
"Great idea," said Leela.
The Aqua Dragons followed Stella to see Madame Octopus.

But Sneaky the Seahorse was scavenging in the seaweed nearby and overheard them.
"I will follow them to Madame Octopus, find out their plan and tell the herd," Sneaky said.

"You must go through Coral Ravine,"
Madame Octopus said. "This route will help
you avoid the seahorses and get you home."
Madame Octopus showed them the route
on a map.
"I've heard about Coral Ravine," Fin said.
"It's dangerous! We could all be crushed to
death."
"Not if you go through quietly," Madame
Octopus said.
Bang! Crash!

"What's that noise?" Leela squealed.
"It's Sneaky the Seahorse," Stella shouted.
"He will warn the rest of the herd,"
Bubbles said.
"We have to stop him from getting away."
Fin darted after Sneaky.

The Aqua Dragons chased Sneaky around the rocks.
Crabby crawled out snapping his claws at them.
He was cross his sleep had been disturbed again.
Crabby grabbed Sneaky in one of his large pincers
and held him high above his shell.
"Keep hold of him," yelled Bubbles.
"Let go of me!" Sneaky struggled to get free from
Crabby's claws.
"All we want to do is get home," Leela said.
"I promise not to tell the rest of the herd if you let
me go," Sneaky said.
The Aqua Dragons glanced at each other.
"O.K." Fin said.
Crabby released Sneaky and he galloped away.

However, when the Aqua Dragons reached Coral Ravine the herd was waiting for them.

"Sneaky must have told the herd," Stella said.

"He lied to us," Fin said.

"How are we going to get home now?" Leela cried.

Bubbles looked around them and spotted the large leaves of the stalked kelp growing at the edge of the ravine.

"Can you snip one of those flat leaves off for us?" he asked Crabby.

Crabby cut the leaf easily with his pincher and while Madam Octopus held the leaf in place, the Aqua Dragons clambered on.

"Release the leaf," Bubbles said. Madam Octopus let go and the leaf glided upwards.

"Bye!" The Aqua Dragons waved goodbye to their new friends.
The leaf drifted to the surface of the water and floated in the gentle current above Coral Ravine.
"They'll be here soon," Sneaky said to the herd of waiting seahorses.
The seahorses did not notice the Aqua Dragons sailing past, above their heads.

The Aqua Dragons sat safely in a warm pool of water on the leaf.
"I can see the mangrove trees." Bubbles pointed.
"We're nearly home," Leela said.
Fin cheered.
They dived off the leaf and swam the rest of the journey home. They were so happy to see their parents and Baby Sandy again.

Can you find all of these things in this book?

☐ Coral

☐ Crab

☐ Mangrove tree roots

☐ Mangrove trees

☐ Octopus

☐ Sea snail

☐ Seaweed

☐ Shoal of fish

☐ Six Aqua Dragons

☐ Starfish

☐ Seahorses

**Other titles in the
Aqua Dragons series:**